Clinton Gregory's SECRET

Bruce Whatley

Abrams Books for Young Readers, New York

Library of Congress Cataloging-in-Publication Data:

Whatley, Bruce.
Clinton Gregory's secret / by Bruce Whatley.
p. cm.
Summary: Clinton Gregory has fantastic adventures every night, from fighting dragons
to flying around the world with his friends, and he keeps each one a secret.
ISBN-13: 978-0-8109-9364-8 (hardcover)
[1. Secrets—Fiction. 2. Dreams—Fiction.] I. Title.
PZ7.W5485Cli 2008
[E]—dc22
2007012760

Book design by Chad W. Beckerman

Published in 2008 by Abrams Books for Young Readers,
an imprint of Harry N. Abrams, Inc.

Printed and bound in China
10 9 8 7 6 5 4 3 2 1

HNA
harry n. abrams, inc.
a subsidiary of La Martinière Groupe
115 West 18th Street
New York, NY 10011
www.hnabooks.com

For Rosie and for making
dreams come true.
—B. W.

Clinton Gregory has a secret.

Actually, Clinton Gregory has at least seven secrets just from last week.

On Monday night,
when everyone else was
asleep, Clinton Gregory . . .
on his own . . . all by himself . . .

wrestled a
dragon named
Gordon!

(Clinton Gregory and Gordon
were really the best of friends.)

On Tuesday night,

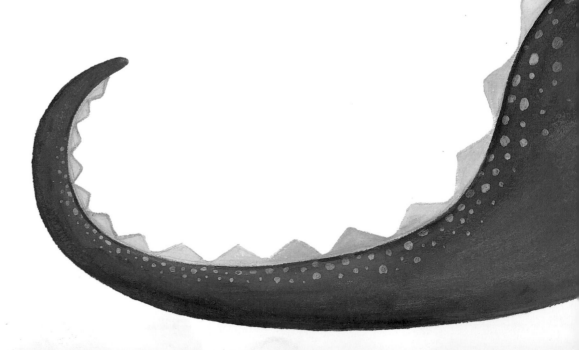

Clinton Gregory played catch with a magic sea horse!

And on Wednesday night,

Clinton
Gregory was
invited to a giant
dinner of boulder peas
and mountain mash.
(No broccoli!)

On Thursday,

it was a busy night for

Clinton Gregory's secrets.

He taught a triceratops
a new trick...

and washed the spots off his tiger.

(Normally, tigers have stripes, but Clinton Gregory's tiger had spots.)

On Friday night,
Clinton Gregory and his friends
danced under the moonlight.

On Saturday,

Clinton Gregory read the evening paper

to a toad who'd lost his glasses.

And on Sunday,

Clinton Gregory and his friends
did nothing.
Nothing much at all.

They made paper hats for
a ship full of pirates . . .

rocketed to the moon and back . . .

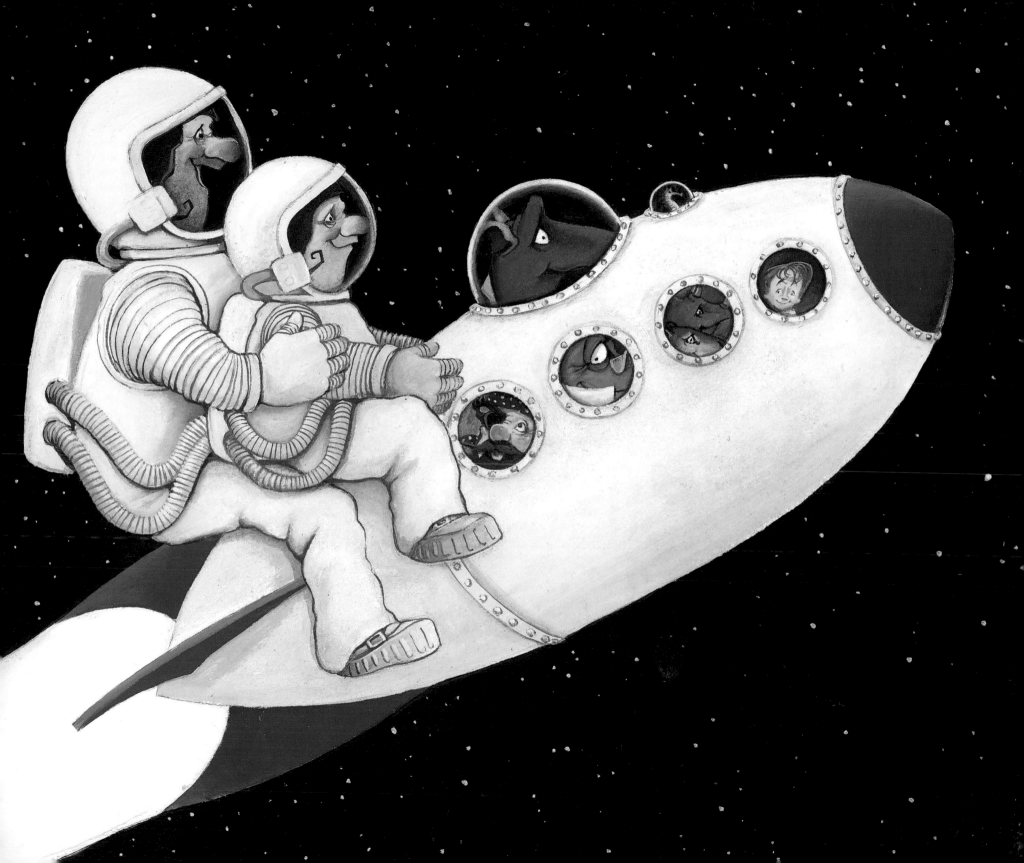

and flew around the world on plates of spaghetti wondering what they would do next week.

And do you know what they decided?

I do.

But it's a secret.